A Collection

of

Inappropriate

Limericks

Malcolm C. Michaels

ISBN –10: 1-91-608901-1

ISBN-13: 978-1-91-608901-3

Dedicated to Dawn, who I have never met. Your arrogance, mean spirit and general horribleness inspired me to write this book.

Sometimes crying or laughing are the only options left, and laughing feels better right now.

Veronica Roth

There once was a doctor from Goole

Specialised in the gastric, no fool.

Made a fortune in bums

Bowels, intestines and tums

And continuing study of stool.

Jerome, a young athlete from Bruges

Had a passion for bobsleigh and luge.

In tight lycra he dressed,

Ladies swooned most impressed

As his bulge was eye wateringly huge.

Flush with cash, dame from North Carolina

Who so craved a sweet custom vagina

Said her beau: "looks fantastic

With your clit made of plastic

And your labia stamped 'made in China'."

Once a farmer of ill reputation

Was accused of such vile molestation

As his pigs looked harassed

And his sheep ran so fast

With a look of intense consternation.

A scoundrel from Bangor I met

Had a shirt that was soaked through with sweat,

As he'd been on the run

From a priest and a nun

And a bishop whose wife he got wet.

This lady with bosoms aplenty

Proved a hit with the men of the gentry.

They succumbed to her wiles

Cheeky winks and wry smiles,

But to church she was oft refused entry.

A young lad that I knew as a senior

He got cancer, I think 'twas leukaemia.

Sadly treatment it failed

He got thinner and paled

And then died and his wife got bulimia.

My dog, my best friend always true

Dedicated to me through and through.

Drunk, I left the door wide

And she ran straight outside

Got ran over and died now I'm blue.

Local vicar round here, who loves choir

Had to quit, giving up his desire.

He could not harmonise

When he lost both his eyes

And his tongue when he fell in a fire.

There's this woman I worked with called Jane

Had a tumour removed from her brain.

She went to celebrate

Thinking "Yeah this is great!"

Got hit, drunk, on way home by a train.

There once was a pervert, Jaffar,

Who with puppies lured kids to his car.

He got caught, locked away

And I'm quite glad to say

He got shanked in the showers, hoorah!

My friend knew a girl, quite the dancer.

Really hot so he thought he'd romance her.

Woo'd her hard, they got wed,

Had two kids then dropped dead

No one knew she'd quite nasty brain cancer.

Mum loved chicken and steak, cheese and bread,

Quite often ate cake in her bed.

Scoffing chocolate and sweeties,

Got real fat, diabetes.

Lost 3 toes then one summer fell dead.

Old love lived alone in a flat

Had no family or friends fancy that.

Banged her head on the ground,

3 weeks 'till she was found

Decomposed, face chewed off by her cat.

A lonely no hoper named Dom

Bought an internet bride, it went wrong.

Because when she appeared

Big hands, penis and beard

Realised he'd clicked girlboybrides.com.

This woman's rich husband was boring.

Old, obese, dull with bad snoring.

Said "Just do what you will

And I'll pick up the bill."

So she shopped, drank and spent her days whoring.

Carl does not like condoms he says

And convinces the ladies he sways.

"'Cos I'm catholic you see

Withdrawal method for me!"

8 kids, 6 mums, one on the way.

Young lovers eloped and got hitched

After time his desires they switched

Now it's gone really bad

And he fancies her dad

'Cos his big hands they have him bewitched.

Barber alas premature

In his loving, his wife needed more.

Said "I need you to last

And not be so damn fast

Cos you're done 'fore I start, that's for sure."

A woman got picked up and drugged

And a good man got beaten and mugged,

But I said to the wife

At least *we've* a good life

She said "you're cold hearted", I shrugged.

Man in charge of the choir last spring

Said he just loves to make the boys sing

"Do it harder and faster!"

Said the old choir master

You really do have a nice ring.

A young man joined up and have no doubt,

A true patriot so he shipped out.

Lost his legs to a mine,

Had some made though, he's fine,

And he always gets parked when he's out.

Cheating wife she got knocked up, oh dear.

Vegan hub sensed that something was queer.

See the couple are white

And the kid's black as night,

So he left her for chicks, meat and beer.

This handsome chap I know romancer

Lovely wife, healthy kids and great dancer.

Had it all so he thought

But it all came to nought

When he died really young of bowel cancer.

These twins at birth were separated

Who later in life met and dated.

They had kids, sad to say

Hip conjoined by the way

Now in freak show they're quite celebrated.

"You're adopted" says father to son,

"And I've just had a chat to your mum.

It's just not working out

We don't want you about,

You're off back to go live with that nun."

Oh the African crisis I never

Have seen such despair no not ever.

Drought, pain, loss, civil war,

HIV, death and more.

But hey, least they've got lovely weather.

A woman I knew, Enid Black

Smoked some weed for an ache in her back,

Then she dabbled in coke

Which she got from "some bloke".

Now spends nights selling boobies for crack.

This baker with skills quite sublime

Made cakes, pies and puddings most fine.

Met a lass, who he wood

With his sensual food.

Said she "your spotted dick is divine!"

Rugged Romeo, wife rather bland

For insurance he schemed and he planned.

But his plot came to nought

By the cops he was caught

Now in prison he gets nightly manned.

Amsterdam...Drugs, whores and beer.

What a weekend he had but I fear

That his wife will discover,

Of his large breasted lover

When the tests come back with gonorrhoea.

A kid from school, who I'd forgotten

Got a vegetable lodged in his bottom.

But he chose to do nowt

And it simply dripped out

A week later when it had gone rotten.

I saw your dad this afternoon

Heard your stomach looks like a balloon

And your bottom has leaked

But your temperature peaked

So I hope that you feel better real soon.

I saw your dad at the garage

Said your scrotum is swollen quite large

Since you went to Bangkok.

I bet it was a shock

When you saw the quite nasty discharge.

A virginal groom of low worth

Just 5 inches, got married in Perth.

Wedding night, all revealed,

With delight his bride squealed

Was not length that he'd measured but girth

Pious church going toff who loved learning

One day felt a rather strong yearning.

He'd enjoyed fifty shades

Now feels wholly depraved

And wakes up every day with loins burning.

My mate's lovely young bride named Jane

Had a tumour alas in her brain.

She died, you can tell,

He'd insured her quite well,

Bought a fantastic villa in Spain.

Distraught groom who was left at the alter

Loved her still so he just would not fault her.

She ran off with her lover

Then got aids from another,

And then died late last year in Gibraltar.

A chubby young pianist called Giles

Got a rather bad case of the piles.

Doc said "don't be so glum -

Pop this cream in your bum,

'Till they're gone just sit carefully and smile."

There's this skinny old postman called pat

Who could eat but could never get fat.

Pies and cakes, buns and sweets,

Vegetables, breads and meats

Had a tapeworm you see, fancy that.

This conservative preacher, John Stead,

Man of God but quite kinky in bed.

By the cleaner discovered

Bound tight, naked and buggered

Purple faced, plastic bag on his head.

Handy plumber from Goole well endowed

Love to take off his clothes in a crowd,

And the ladies he'd please

As it hung to his knees

Hand on hips, legs akimbo, so proud.

This vicar from Grimsby most hated,

Spent a celibate life most frustrated

Unless you count the young boys

Who he used as his toys

'Till they caught him and now he's castrated.

A hillbilly chap, quite obese

One day covered his sister in grease

From her toes to her head

Then he took her to bed.

She gave birth to his daughter and niece.

Each morning I look at your smiles

Even though you both put us through trials.

How your mother she bore you

And I simply adore you

So does mum though you did give her piles.

A handsome poor priest name of Chad

Found that boobies they made him most glad.

So he gave up the life

Found a super-hot wife

With big lips, curvy hips and rich dad.

Muslim chap hailing from York

Had a secretive yearning for pork.

So he gave up the life

Shaved, de-shrouded his wife

Gorging bacon and beans with a spork.

There's this Hindu lass hailing from Neath

Caused her family much heartache and grief,

And dishonour and shame

To the family name

As she sneakily gorged on roast beef.

A Jewish lass, Emily Fisk

Her eternal life greatly at risk

With shrimp mussels and cod

She'd offended her God

Now each day she eats hot lobster bisque.

A trusting young boyfriend from Rhyll

Thought his girlfriend was still on the pill.

She'd forgotten to take,

What a costly mistake,

Now they're 18 with twins, what a thrill.

Chap from Mosul played drums in a band

So the Taliban cut off each hand.

But it all worked out fine

Said his wife, "it's divine

'Cos for scratching my back your hook's grand."

This young suicide bomber named Bert

So frustrated, his testicles hurt.

Blew himself into three

For the virgins you see

He was promised – tall, short, round and pert.

There once was a man from Japan

Loved a lady but also a man.

Got the best of both worlds

When he found this Thai girl

Called petunia, but used to be Stan.

This young kid who was rather forlorn

Found a stash of his father's best porn.

Now he's happy and glad

But his father's quite mad

'cos the pages are sticky and torn.

A house wife from Bradford called Jess

Caught her hub one day wearing a dress.

How it made her eyes pop

So he's having the op,

Now her Trevor's becoming a Tess.

There once was a farmer of note

Had a thing, quite obscene, with a goat.

Neighbours frowned, disapproved

As they did acts quite lewd

"We're quite happy" he said, quote, unquote.

Child I know finds Santa scary

With his beard so big white and quite hairy,

And his bulging great sack

And his lock picking knack.

Christmas eve, keeps the lights on quite wary.

A quite lovely temptress from Dover

Loved to frolic and roll in the clover.

She would lie in the dew

With a fellow or two

Caught a chill, went without a pullover.

Hungry butcher from Leeds who loved pies,

Can't resist them, though trust me tries.

Now his belly's quite round

And his man boobs profound

And you should see the size of his thighs.

Young wild bloke with a taste for wild nights

Bought a hooker in basque and black tights.

Unprotected he played

Wife found out that he'd strayed

Came home scratched and all covered in bites.

A Peruvian who so loved his llama,

When it died shipped it to an embalmer.

When returned he was thrilled

Sexy posed and quite filled,

Now he spoons it at night, sans pyjama.

Once a naturist nun loved a giggle

And to dance and my word did she jiggle.

Pendulous she would swing

Heaving breasts, quite the thing

And her bottom quite wildly she'd wiggle.

There once was a priest from Belize

Whose penis hung down to his knees

But it only got used

On the boys he abused

Gets beat nightly in jail, I'm quite pleased.

A handy young camper from Kent

Spent his weekends outdoors in a tent,

But a wind came on through

Ripped his home clean in two

Left him soaked and confused, poles quite bent.

Nasty robber from Torremolinos

Stole to get cash for his penis

To enlarge was his wish

But the products are pish

Now he's locked up in jail with men heinous.

'My friend' watches far too much telly

Middle aged, double chins and round belly,

Legs and arms got quite thick

Now he can't see his dick

And his man boobs they jiggle like jelly.

A husband one day proclaimed dead

Seems his wife shot him right through the head.

On his phone saw a text:

"Banged your sister, you're next!"

Really made quite a mess of the bed.

Farmers wife with a craving for men

Got caught cheating again and again,

Hub quite angry threw fits

Then he chopped her to bits

Fed her parts to the pigs in his pen.

There lived a young chap in Caracas

Who had swollen, enlarged, quite red knackers.

Thought he'd best see the doc

Who grabbed hold of his cock

And gave them a shake like maracas.

This mechanic from North Carolina

Had the hots for a big burly miner,

Left his family in shock

When he 'fessed "it's the cock,

I just like it way more than vagina."

A builder from Cork name of Shamus

Had a monstrous and cavernous anus.

In his bottom he placed

Knives, forks, bowls cups and plates

Now he's massive on YouTube, quite famous.

There once was a chap from Milan

Had a thing for his best mate Paul's gran.

Craved her wrinkly bits

And her pendulous tits

Of her saggy old thighs, a big fan.

An irregular builder from Goole

Bought a potion to soften his stool.

He strained with a large load

And his bowels did explode.

Don't gamble with farts. That's the rule.

A woman from Selby quite cute

Survived mostly on vegies and fruit.

But most every fart

Would result in a shart,

Just imagine the stress of each toot.

Horny lonely young vet from Uganda

At the zoo fell in love with a panda.

Craved its fluffy white thighs

And it's come to be eyes

Got him rather aroused, double hander!

Dairy sales man who worked in Calcutta

Had a mind that was oft in the gutter.

Home he'd go self to please

Rub his bollocks with cheese

And his nipples he'd smother in butter.

There once was an old man from Chile

Now you're thinking I'll write of his willy

That would be rather sick

To write odes of old dick

I'm more grown up than that, don't be silly…

Bloke next door has this girlfriend, most flirty

Who based on the noise, gets quite dirty.

"God that stings" through the walls

Heard him shout, slips and falls

Bangs his head, seems she's also quite squirty.

Single bloke I know lives with no cares.

Drunk encounters each night, unawares.

Meets this lass in Bangkok

Got a terrible shock,

Didn't see Adam's apple, he swears.

There once was a wife, sweet Theresa

Who alas was quite prone to a seizure.

Though sometimes during sex

He'd not know what was next

She'd vibrate, hub would squeal, a real pleaser!

There once lived a lady named Jane

Who so loved to dance out in the rain.

Got a cold, then a sniff

Then pneumonia, quite stiff

Now lies dead and no coat was to blame.

An alpha male type, macho guy

One day realised he may well be bi.

Now he's down on the dock's

And he's gobbling on cocks,

Sailor three ways and all sorts he'll try.

Saw on Facebook you're not feeling good,

Please indulge me this thought if you would.

Get your arse off to bed

If you're feeling so dead

'stead of posting dumb updates, I would!

Young and single and sexually free

Unprotected you play cos you see.

You were really quite thick

Now you're grabbing youre dick

Std feels like fire when you pee.

Hurt your wrist now you're feeling forlorn.

Is it twisted or ligaments torn?

Now you know that we all

Think it's not from a fall

But from wanking all night watching porn.

Oh poor lamb heard you've got gonorrhoea

And the symptoms they seem quite severe.

Now it burns when you piss

You'd not bargained on this

When you paid for that hooker, oh dear.

I heard you're quite bloated today

And your stomach's all growly you say.

Just give in, let it out

Unleash hell have no doubt

You'll feel better quite soon, fart away.

There once was a hot-shot, Don T

Who its rumoured has showered in pee

Let it run down his back

Twixt his legs, through his crack,

Hence the tone of his skin, don't you see?

There once was a gardener from Leeds

Had some real dark and rather sick needs.

Shouted "bring me a goat

Two small dogs and a stoat

And a full yard of glass anal beads."

A buxom young barwench of olde

Had a knack of securing men's gold.

Of her assets quite proud

She'd stand out in a crowd

End even more so when it's cold.

Each December we put up a tree,

Decorate it with oh so much glee.

Then we watch as it dies

As we gorge on mince pies

Christmas pudding, cold turkey and brie.

My poor neighbour addicted to crack

Pimped himself cos he couldn't go back

To his family and wife

Though he missed his old life

He was also quite hooked on ball sack.

There's this man I met on a kibbutz

Had a tumour on one of his nuts.

Like a grapefruit it swelled

Wouldn't cease and he yelled

"Oh god please cut it off, hurts too much."

There was a young man from China

Met this lass with a massive vagina

He would rattle inside.

She would say "It's so wide,

But was tighter way back, and much finer."

An endowed entertainer called Scott

Has a dick he could tie in a knot.

Animals he could make

Dogs, swords, flowers or snake,

Some girls found it incredibly hot.

Lad I know, poor thing - anus quite wrecked

He hit forty so prostate got checked.

Turned out loved it so much

Craved it poked, drilled and touched

Far more pleasure that one might expect.

Oh sweet Jesus heard you have ebola

From the trip that you took to Angola.

Your insides turned to mush

And they ran out your tush,

Get well soon but I'm not coming over.

A quite curious frustrated vicar

Said "I need to get laid" on the liquor

But he's dull and no looker

So he's out with a hooker

With big boobs cos they get him off quicker.

Politician in Lords, landed gentry

Loved to instruct young boys by the plenty

Every night as a rule

He'd head down to the school

And insists "Open up, give me entry!"

A young Muslim was really quite shaken

When he realised he rather loved bacon.

He tried to be devout

But he loved chops and snout.

Judgement day he is sure to be shakin'.

Crazy rugby fan Jennifer Smalls,

For big men in tight shorts climbed the walls.

And she couldn't resist

The intense violent hits

And the wonderfully misshapen balls.

A young prudish chap found it perverted

When his bride screamed, eyes closed and then squirted.

He thought she was possessed

When he witnessed the mess

As she thrashed about, nipples inverted.

A fine gent who went off of the rails

Whose dark deeds insignificant pail

When compared to his wife

Cos she's living the life

Having threesomes with clowns in North Wales.

Bloke I know big fan of one-night stands

Got quite drunk and as part of plans

Took a lass to his place

Now has scabs on his face

And his knob and a rash on his hands.

This Greek man I know Theo Grafitis

Filled his face with cakes biscuits and sweeties

Grew progressively wider

On sweet apple cider.

Nearly died, lost his toes, diabetes.

Friend of mine had this girlfriend called Lucy.

Rather thin, none the less quite a beauty.

Fed her bagels and chips

Ribs cakes burgers and dips

Now she's perfect, round curvy and juicy.

Met a young single woman called Wendy

Who in bed was fantastically bendy

After one or two beers

Had her legs round her ears.

With the chaps was incredibly trendy.

Once a lady of quite ill repute

Played the penis just like 'twas a flute.

She would give the girls tips

On the best use of lips

And then strum it like playing a lute.

Wild commuter, perverted young Justin

In packed carriages often found thrusting

Against strangers unknown

He would shudder and moan

And head home quite aroused his loins busting.

This brave gourmet loved curry and spice,

Ate madras, korma, bhajis and rice.

Then he started to sweat

'Till he was dripping wet.

God the state of the toilet, not nice.

Buxom lactating woman from Leeds,

Had some twisted and quite kinky needs.

It would make her knees buckle

When she watched a pig suckle

On her nipples, she loves how it feeds.

Carl, a man well-endowed down below

Met a lass who was quite keen to blow

All his cash on nice things

Gucci bags, diamond rings.

You expected much worse there, I know. ;)

A good Christian man from Geelong

Who enjoyed to put on his wife's thong.

Slipped and fell, it's no laugh,

Cut his balls clean in half

Now soprano at church sings along.

Friend of mine caught his wifey in bed

With a big burly fellow called Ted

Who was quite well endowed

And incredibly proud.

Took the house, car and both kids instead.

There once was a vet born in France,

Gerbils caused quite a stir in his pants.

Rabbits caused a cold sweat

And his trousers got wet,

Fondles hamsters if given a chance.

Once a husband caught aids from a hooker

Quite infected but still quite a looker.

Gave his wife it, she died

And their graves the kids cried.

On his gravestone it read, "What a fucker."

Rich financier born in Sri Lanka

Who wrote poems, quite odd for a banker

He would take such delight

In his form oh so tight

How he revelled in haiku and tanka.

I once met a farmer called Phil

Bought a bride on the web from Brazil.

When she landed such shock

Massive balls and a cock

It worked out though, she's hung, what a thrill.

There's this vicar, Jeff, who comes from Cannes

Who when drunk went to bed with a man.

He's now happy it seems

With the man of his dreams

Left the church, toured the world in a van.

Heard you're spending some time on the loo

And your whole house it smells just like poo

And you really can't think

With your head in the sink

As it's coming out of that end too.

Seems your boob job it went quite awry

When you look at them you just start to cry,

'Cos they're both different sizes

And they're full of surprises

As one nipple looks like a pork pie.

Stay in bed as I know you're unwell

There's a discharge, a rash - must be hell.

Get some shots, you'll be fine

It will heal up in time

And perhaps it will no longer smell.

Friend of mine met a woman, Denise,

Super-hot but alas smelled like cheese.

Tried quite hard, could not bed her

As she smelled just like cheddar

Gorgonzola, blue Danish and brie's.

There once was a lad, quite humongous.

Never bathed, in his rolls he grew fungus.

In his chins you'd find mould,

Sweat would pool in each fold,

In his crack nasty filth in abundance.

Once a hungry young lady called Kate

Who would eat every crumb on her plate.

She would nibble from others,

From her parents and brothers,

Now quite round and she can't find a date.

Ballet dancer who got rather plump

So much so that she barely could jump.

All the cookies and pies

They went straight to her thighs

When she did, she came down with a thump.

Once a gent with a craving for women

Went to watch them and spied on them swimming.

He emerged, they screamed "weirdo!"

At the bulge in his speedo.

Didn't help, the lip licking and grinning.

Fan of X-files insisted he'd been

By some aliens, sucked up in a beam,

Stretched his bottom quite wide

As they probed deep inside

The poor chap what they did was obscene.

There once hailed a priest from Manilla

Who turned out was a serial killer.

Though on Sundays he'd rest

With the saved and the blessed.

Then on Monday, kill whores, what a thriller.

Hungry woman quite fond of baguette

Just the shape brought her out in a sweat.

The soft inner, hard crust

Filled her mind with such lust

And a footlong, well that made her wet.

There once lived a man in Phuket

Kept an elephant calf as a pet

Treat it rather quite bad

It grew large and got mad

Squashed him flat, left a smear, rather wet.

An old lady who rather loved cats

Lived alone in a tall block of flats

Died alone at her place

And the cats ate her face

Decomposed, then was fed on by rats.

Friend of mine on vacation in Delhi

Drank the water and god a bad belly.

He would cry scream and shout

As he turned inside out

Quite disgusting and rather quite smelly.

My mate Albert, think he's from Peru

Without pork he simply could not do.

He could not live without

Daily servings of snout,

Curly tails, pointy ears, trotters too.

Bestiality fan from Tibet

Would see kittens, break out in a sweat.

She once fondled a puppy,

Rubbed her boobs on a guppy

Let a couple of rats make her wet.

A young person unsure of his sex

Found the subject intense, left him vexed.

Was it her, it or him,

Mr, miss, sir or shim

Gender pronouns really are complex.

A girl name of Kirsty McWhirter

Great in bed and a bit of a squirter

She would cry out your name

Just as if quite in pain

By the noise you would think that you'd hurt her.

There once was a teacher named Tash

Who one day she did sprout a moustache.

Cross her lip it did wend

And curl up at the end,

Joined the circus and made loads of cash.

Once I met a young named Bert

Loved his milk cows so much that it hurt

Went too far, made me shudder

What he did with that udder.

Let's just say that it caused quite the squirt.

A quite wonderful dancer called Shirley

Whose pubes were quite thick and most curly.

It was full and so plush

A most seventies bush

Who'd have thought for a creature most girly.

Stern faced prudish young woman named Jude

Had a belly that seemed to protrude.

It turned out to be gas

Cos she not let her ass

Pass wind as he found it quite rude.

My mate worked with a woman called Cath,

Didn't shower and seldom did bath.

God the stench from her pits

Tits and rank naughty bits.

It's not funny you so shouldn't laugh

There once was a baker call Ned

Quite a perv, things he did with the bread.

Doughnut holes...yeah believe it

Used his bits to achieve it

Late at night he'd take croissants to bed.

This adventurous lady called Mary

Who's back was incredibly hairy

And her arms legs and tush

Shoulders chest neck and bush

In a two-piece was really quite scary.

Loves young dream at the alter they stand.

The wedding she wanted, quite grand

Three hours later all tears

Full of champagne and beers

Bridesmaid caught with his knob in her hand.

Chap I know met a lass from Djibouti

Eyes like sapphires and lips red like rubies

Said he so loved her mind

But quite adored her behind

And was rather obsessed with her boobies.

A comely barmaid from Mauritius

Proclaimed "Semen is oh so delicious

And so good for my skin

And it keeps me quite thin

Full of protein and very nutritious."

Once a lover quite fond of romance

Took a buxom young girl to a dance

He was charming and sweet

Swept her right off her feet

All a plan to get into her pants.

Fred, a talented potter from Crete,

Had a quite kinky craving for feet,

How he craved toes and heels

Cos it gave him sex feels

And the odour he loved, oh so sweet.

Friend of mine met a woman called Wendy

Who he claimed was incredibly bendy

To applause, whoops and cheers

Legs tucked behind her ears.

Oh my god! The photos he once sent me.

Once in Rhyll lived a plumber called Andy

Had a wife who when drunk got quite randy

She was game, full of wine

And on beer quite divine

But my god what a tramp when on brandy.

Mourning widow in black at the grave

For her husband did cry, being brave.

But when home she'd rejoice

At the fear in his voice

When with candle his head she did stave.

Chap I know met this lass on the net

Got him hot and into quite a sweat.

The reveal was a shock

Turned out she had a cock

(and some big hairy balls I would bet).

Heard a tale of a quite horny vicar

Met a nun and he wanted to lick her

From her head to her shins

Then forgive all her sins

Then smoke fags and do shots of string liquor.

Once a preacher condemned fornication

And booze, porn, drugs and wild masturbation.

Then was caught by the press

In lipstick, wig and dress

Giving hand jobs to men near the station.

A straight lad thought that he would perhaps

Enjoy butt sex then his sphincter collapsed.

Oh my god came the shout

As his insides dripped out

It's like someone turned on the shit taps.

A gym bunny, just one of the boys

Wanted mass so he turned to the 'roids.

As his pecs grew quite thick

He lost sight of his dick,

He don't care 'cos he flexes with poise.

Preacher shouts "By God surely I'm blessed."

Yet at home you would find him cross dressed.

French cut panties all lace

Basque pulled taught at the waist

Really loves how it shows off his chest.

Once a churchgoing builder from Leeds

Had no kids as he had wonky seeds.

And his wife's now devout

With her belly stuck out

"…Miracle, I'm no trollop" she pleads.

A poor beauty, but so very hot

Wealthy suitors lined up hot to trot.

Married rich, left her mums,

Now she's back in the slums

She got fat, he got rid in a shot.

Lonely shepherd loved poetry deep

Would wax lyrically about his sheep.

Though he went way too far

Dressing one in a bra

And then spooning her there in her sleep.

Heavy drinker of scant recollection

Could not recall that he'd had an erection

Inside a fresh hot dog bun,

He'd accosted a nun.

Now he's locked up for his own protection

There once was an artist form Doncaster

Who screamed and begged "baby go faster!"

She could not get enough

Of his lovely man stuff

Had a copy of it made of plaster.

A fat baker quite fond of cream cake

And sweet treats, for their goodness he'd ache.

Gorged on chocolate and choux

Gateaux and jam tarts too

And meringues, well they'd make his moobs shake.

An old woman claimed she was the best

And was crowned 1920's best chest.

Now it's all gone awry

And they hang to her thigh,

Yet way back, boy, she sure filled a vest.

There once was a woman from Spain

Who delighted to dance in the rain.

She went out in fake tan

But came in rather wan

As alas it all washed down the drain.

A lass angry and jilted from Reading

Burst in, interrupted a wedding.

Said "last night this here groom

Took me back to his room."

So the bride's brothers kicked the chaps head in.

Ugly bloke, oh so hairy and squat

Got this girlfriend, incredibly hot

Thought he made the girl itch

He was really quite rich

Seems that helped her like him quite a lot.

There once was a lad name Horatio

Mathematician, quite fond of fellatio.

With his mouth he would please

When he's down on his knees,

Tell you how much he took and the ratio.

Worn out wife who was tired of life,

Boorish husband and just endless strife,

So ungrateful and rude

Violent bad attitude,

Cut him up with a large kitchen knife.

Friend of mine wed this chap, quite the bloke,

Things got stale and it wasn't no joke.

He said "Let's spice things up

- watch 2 girls and 1 cup."

Now he's single, she's back at her folks.

Once a fair faced young damsel from Gwent

At a festival went to her tent

With a handsome young buck

Who it seems was in luck

Then watched cold play, smoked weed, rather spent.

Lonely chap on the net bought a Russian

Rather forward she left the lad blushing.

She'd explode like a geyser

The more he would please her

He'd be really quite soaked from the gushing.

Cheese loving nudist from Caracas

Thought he had something wrong with his knackers.

Thought perhaps it was crabs

Or some nasty dried scabs

But turns out was just crumbs from the crackers.

An incestuous man, fan of twister

Darkest urge as he played with his sister.

Remarked "oh my dear Julie

You're so supple quite truly."

Late that night on his palm quite the blister.

Respected man of esteemed reputation

Quite addicted to wild masturbation.

The real thing he would shirk

Instead content to jerk

And enjoy solo gratification.

Master baker used iced fingers

To seduce two sisters, both cute gingers.

Should have known they'd find out

And they did, have no doubt

As he gave them both aids, and that lingers.

Politician of high social station

Took some tablets. Severe constipation.

Halfway through a debate

Such an explosive fate

Shat his pants live in front of the nation.

A fat father of girth quite unique,

Out of breath when he walked, couldn't speak.

So he cut down on lard

Trained incredibly hard.

Fell down dead, heart attack, in first week.

A young man, with good looks by the plenty

Slept with hundred from eighteen to twenty,

Twice as many to thirty

More to forty, so dirty,

But now no more, he's spent and quite empty.

Narcoleptic chain smoker, Belinda

Nodded off, burnt her house to a cinder.

Now she's trying to make cash

On the street selling ass

To the men that she locates on tinder.

Sex mad virile young stud name of Darren,

He divorced, said his missus was barren.

Try as hard as he could

Was his sperm that was dud,

She remarried, 3 kids, Joe, Zak, Aaron.

Clad in white, batsman quite fond of cricket

So much so he would dance down the wicket

And with joyous delight

In the sun shining bright

Pull a stump out, caress it and lick it.

Daring lass from the banks of the Humber

Who did quite shocking things with cucumber.

What she did with a squash

Made you wince and say gosh,

But oh how you'd kill for her number.

Hear that thing on your leg has got worse

You should probably go see a nurse

Cos it smells really off

And you've got a bad cough

Or we'll soon see you off in a hearse.

Master builder, an eye for perfection

Met an architect fond of inspection.

Day by day how he woo'd

Took her out for some food

And insisted "Come, see my erection."

Veterinarian, fond of his horse,

Was accused of such vile intercourse.

Though there was just no proof

Save some jizz on a hoof,

He denied it and showed no remorse.

There once was a chap from Fflint

Sold his body because he was skint,

You'd be shocked at the cash

That he got for his ass

Opinion was it was quite mint.

A friend of mine does like to gush

Bout his lady friends wild pubic bush.

Extolls its shag, thick and nice

Says she back combs it twice

And conditions it to keep it lush.

Twas a woman who loved with devotion,

Said it's not size that matters but motion.

Though alas in the wet,

He would toil, he would sweat,

Tiny boat set adrift on vast ocean.

Well to do wife screwed her trainer

At her wish he choked, spanked and restrained her,

But it went all awry,

Asphyxiated did die

Now he wishes he'd been an abstainer.

A god-fearing vicar called Martin

So loved Jesus but couldn't stop farting.

He would speak of god's grace,

Let one go and the place,

Starts to gag, congregations' eyes smarting.

A cross eyed young dentist called Steven

Had teeth that stuck out, most uneven.

He could not understand

When he smiled, shook their hand,

And they suddenly upped and were leaving.

There's this vegetable seller Lynette

Who sees marrows, goes red starts to sweat.

Gets embarrassed and flustered

Be they red, green or mustard,

Lost control one time with a courgette.

Hot gym goer who so enjoyed Monday

Lycra clad, pulse would race such a fun day,

He would get little done

Open mouthed, drooling some,

For the ladies you see, it was buns day.

Once a scholar of highest esteem

Oxford dean and old friend of the Queen,

Though behind the closed doors

A purveyor of whores

Big fan of being spanked and whipped queen.

Woeful lonely young barman called Bertie

Placed an ad, for a lass, "rather dirty,

Some big dildos you're packing,

Into kink and tarmacking,

Intense bdsm, and face squirting."

A hot-blooded young baker called Dicky

Had a thing for hot bread and so quick he

Would fondle baguette

Blush and stammer and sweat

And his fingers would end up quite sticky.

A deflated young woman did snigger

Tinder date, she had hoped for much bigger.

She persisted and tried

But was unsatisfied,

Barely started, then over, hair trigger.

An accountant who defeated cancer

Said "I'll be an exotic male dancer.

Loving life is a must

I shall work on my thrust

A spray tan and gold thong is the answer."

There once was a singleton, Kate,

Met a tinder lad, went on a date,

She felt rather aggrieved

His pics seems, did deceive

'Cos a headshot didn't show his huge weight.

Veterinarian fond of iguanas

Gazed with lust at frogs, monkeys and llamas.

He'd come over all queer

At the site of a deer

And just couldn't be trusted by farmers.

Geriatric old artist called Jude

Liked to walk round the house in the nude.

Paints still life in the buff

Neighbour cried, "Please, enough"

Close the curtains, your plums look most stewed."

"Check your prostate" my friend's wife insisted.

So he went, pants dropped, face red and twisted.

He enjoyed it so much

And went home and begged such

That each night he's oiled up, roughly fisted.

Once a booze-hound with vague recollection

From a night out brought home an infection.

Blamed it all on the booze

As it started to ooze

"Looks like herpes" said the doc on inspection.

Newly married, bride said "You need practice"

She professed to be pure, such an actress.

Would have ended in tears

Had he known through the years

She'd enjoyed far more pricks than a cactus.

Lad I know, met a girl, made a pass

Problem was uncontrollable gas.

Though quite perfectly suited

They'd make love and he tooted

Now he's single, well you can't blame the lass.

Heard you're down in the dumps - hugs and smiles

Seems you have a bad case of the piles

And they're hanging like grapes

And your butt really gapes

Eat more bran they'll be fine in a while.

A hormonal young teenager Ricky

Who awoke every day rather sticky

And each morning's first task

Was a pretty tough ask

Unglue him from his sheets - rather tricky.

This sad husband who hailed from Phuket

Every day he would drink to forget.

How his wife would cavort

With men at the resort,

Hated swimming but loved to get wet.

Man I know goes on every diet

Fasting, juice, Atkinson's – oh he'll try it.

See it seems to not matter

Just gets fatter and fatter,

Raids the fridge every night – he'll deny it.

Devout god fearing vicar form Neath

Who gave up on her Christian belief.

Thoughts of wuthering heights

Kept her up every night

Oft cavorted way up on the heath.

There once was a woman from France

Asked a baker to go to a dance

As she really did want

His baguette and croissant

And his perfectly shaped vol-aux-vents.

Dandy lover, convinced he was gifted

Said "I'm surely your best" and insisted

"Baby I'll make you moan"

But if only he'd known

During sex to ex loves she oft drifted.

Heard your gastric bypass went quite well

Though you're starving and grumpy as hell.

Silver lining they say

You'll lose weight day by day

And you'll sweat less so maybe won't smell.

Friend of mine hated Tuesday, such dread

So he refused to get out of his bed.

To sleep Monday, forlorn,

And get up Wednesday morn

And between under blankets instead.

Linda, this woman from Maine

Loved her dog but it drove her insane.

Ate her chairs and the sofa

Soiled her husband bill's loafer,

Doleful eyes insist he's not to blame.

Stingy man who would give nought to charity

Had a moment of soul-searching clarity

Gave up all he possessed

To the poor did divest

All his goods to try make up disparity.

A hardworking hooker, not picky

About who'd she'd get hot and quite sticky.

She jerked Nig, Claude and Fred

To big Dave she gave head

Slept with Tommy, Giles, Mark, Luke and Ricky.

Large lad, Mark, who thought "well alrighty"

When alone would slip on his wife's nighty.

Loved the soft silken feel,

Made him quiver and squeal,

Lace clad 300 pounds, most unsightly.

Oh you poor little bugger, so sad,

Heard your piercing's infected quite bad

And it's likely you'll lose it,

Lesson learned - don't abuse it,

How you'll miss what you lost that you had.

Girl I knew back in school – Afrikaner,

Could do quite awesome things with banana.

They would make your eyes water,

Really not sure who taught her

If her mother knew it would alarm her.

Religious perv hailing from Gent

Gave up masturbating for lent.

Lasted 'till the first morn

He succumbed to some porn

By eleven was rather quite spent.

There once was a vet from Manilla

Fell in love with an 8ft gorilla

Found it ever so grand

Silver coat and big hands

Things it did with bananas would thrill her

Once a scholar somewhat of a sceptic

When his girlfriend said she's epileptic.

Well he ended up dead,

Had a fit giving head,

Bit it off, got infected, quite septic.

Rotund builder from old Billericay

In hot weather turned red and quite sticky.

Sweat would run down his back

And then pool in his crack,

Thighs would chafe and his pits, god how icky.

My wife's friend met this hottie called Trevor

Quite a dish but alas not too clever.

Abs of steel, jiggly pecs

Oh my god and the sex

Always game, here or there or wherever.

Tis a rule when the romance is starting

Star crossed lovers refrain please from farting,

But a month or two in

He'll explode with a grin

In her face with such might, her bangs parting.

An adventurous hubby called Ted

Liked to wear women's nickers to bed,

Though his wife seemed to care

He looked better than her,

Killed the mood and the moment quite dead.

Star crossed lovers and destined by fate

A connection so deep and most great

Then he let himself go

So she slept with his bro

And ran off with the dad of his mate.

Giles, a fine tailor from France

When alone he would take off his pants

For he could not resist

The sweet lure of the wrist

As he had little luck with romance.

Vegan lass with a vegetable fetish

Saw a marrow and got rather wettish.

Zucchini clasped in each hand

She would loudly demand,

"In my bottom please place a crisp lettuce!"

"Damned men" said a woman from Texas

"They're like dogs, and oh my how they vex us.

They won't leave you alone

'Till they've buried the bone

Disappear and then won't even text us."

Friend of mine had a girlfriend called Wendy

Into swinging she said "It's quite trendy"

He would idly stand by

Whilst each penis she'd try

Didn't last, though she's still an attendee.

Horny newlywed man from Mauritius

Told his wife that his jizz was nutritious

And quite good for her skin

And would keep her quite thin

Raised an eyebrow, not daft, quite suspicious.

Fed up bloke who packed up and moved west

Met this lass with a pendulous chest,

Quite the largest he'd felt

Which she tucked in her belt

Helps her posture, gives her back a rest.

There hailed a young woman from Ghana

Would do quite shocking things with banana.

She would use up a bunch

Between breakfast and lunch

Though she said its ok, they won't harm her

Deviant vet rather dark and malicious

He found hamsters and rabbits delicious,

Dog he found a bit tough,

Not like parrot or dove

And oh how he liked cats, nutritious!

Gardner born just outside Harrow

Had to cart his testes in a barrow.

But it gets even worse,

'Tis a terrible curse,

Has a penis the size of a marrow.

A quite flexible chap from Burundi

Was a fellow from Thursday to Sunday

Then some blusher, a tuck,

Padded bra and good luck,

Was a woman first thing on the Monday.

Straight laced husband with waning resistance

He succumbed to a chap who's persistence

Saw his nights and most days

Filled with sensual way

Now he can't walk without some assistance.

Fearsome Viking with passion and yearning

For the arts, dancing, poems and learning.

Sadly had to forego,

Tis the season you know

For the pillaging, raping and burning.

Friend of mine has a proctologist

Who shirks fingers, instead uses fist.

Claims its truly divine

Has it done all the time,

He first tried it in Amsterdam pissed.

Scottish musician Roddy McDougall

Rugged looks, kind and handsome, quite frugal.

How the ladies would wilt

At the sight of his kilt

At his impressive bagpipes and bugle.

There's a plumber I know that pees sitting

As the end of his dick has a split in

And it sprays uncontrolled

And he can't hit the bowl

Just no chance of him aiming and hitting.

Amorous vicar woke up on a Sunday

At his cold wife winked "Hey is it fun day?"

She declined his request

And insisted at best

A quick hand job on three weeks from Monday.

Young couple, love's garden were tending

Every moment each day they were spending

And their love grew and grew

Oh the things they would do

Though she drew a clear line at rear ending.

Devout chap once in Bangkok did wonder

Why the ladies packed hot trouser thunder.

Grew up Christian, protected

So he never expected.

But too late, went ahead, pleasant blunder.

Grace, a lady of charms, poise and style

With a wink and caress would beguile.

Round her finger she wrapped

Foolish men, quite entrapped,

And the things she could do with a smile.

Pyromaniac nympho Melinda

Snagged a willing young fireman from tinder.

As she reached for the lube

Candle fell on his pubes

Burnt his scrotum and knob to a cinder.

Body builder tight bodied and ripped

On his torso worked hard but legs skipped.

His top half was gigantic

Though a breeze made him frantic

As unbalanced he wobbled and tripped.

Boastful cad from just south east of Perth

Boasted he had great length and such girth.

But it ended in tears,

Dropped his pants on the beers,

"Hey it's cold" he protested to mirth.

Wicked charlatan, not reverential

Said "I'll tell folks god's quite existential

And that yeah, I'm his son,

Had a thing with my mum,

It's sure to make cash, has potential."

There's this kinky young barman from Crete

Got turned on at the sight of the feet.

Lost his mind at nice heels,

Arches so made him squeal,

The aroma...he exploded...so sweet!

Stats scientist hailed from the states

Compiled stats on each one of his dates,

Compared each on a chart

To find what set them apart,

Still a virgin unlike all his mates.

Married chap who, it seems, he did wonder

About porn that he watched, "chocolate thunder."

He then hungered and craved

The dark python quite shaved,

Till he had it - it tore him asunder.

A quite fortunate lad born in harrow,

A urethra quite long but so narrow.

He could go all damn night

With no ending in sight

Sixty-nine, doggy style and wheel barrow.

Nervous Ned, with a weak constitution

Spent much time on his daily ablutions,

He would wipe, scrub and clean

'Till his bottom did gleam

And was free from unsightly pollutions.

Playboy woke up scared n screamin'

As he thought that he'd ran out of semen.

With a groan and a thrust

Just a moan and some dust,

Double checked, such relief, only dreamin'.

Forlorn poor lover with erectile woes,

Bad sleep walker as well, as it goes.

Took blue Viagra pill

Down the stairs he did spill.

Broke his shoulder, his cock and three toes.

Normal chap from the banks of the Humber

Met this bloke and he gave him his number.

How his jaw hit the floor

When he knocked at the door

With some rope, Vaseline and cucumber.

Dedicate vet, loved work intensely

Got quite heated, loved gerbils immensely.

Hamsters so made her sweat,

Guinea pigs made her wet,

And with rabbits gets quite over friendly.

There's this lass from the south of the Andes

Got aroused on a couple of shandies.

When on wine, lust divine,

Glass of port, 69,

And my god what she'd do when on brandies.

On a health kick this bloke from Mauritius

Drank his own sperm, claimed it was nutritious,

And so good for his skin

And it kept him quite thin.

Milked himself three times daily. Delicious.

Greedy Fred, quite incredibly fat

Rather lonely got himself a cat

But one day when it slept

He sat down, and then wept

As the poor little bugger went splat.

Cheeky chap with a loin stiffening craving

For large women with beards he'd start raving.

He'd explode with a splash

At a chick with a 'tash,

Hairy chins get him badly behaving.

Wicked dentist with cravings malicious

Found his knocked-out patients quite delicious,

He would oft go to town

With his trousers pulled down

They'd come round mouth wide, unsuspicious.

Wayward student not great at biology

Should have researched 'fore attending proctology.

Turned out quite the surprise

When doc said, open wide

For his cold hands, offered an apology.

Handsome, suave self-confessed lady killer

Met a lady boy when in Manilla.

Soon the roles were reversed,

Penetrated he cursed,

Though he went back for more, such a thriller.

An industrious hobo from Kent

Had no home, not a box nor a tent,

Sold his bottom for cash

Round his mouth, nasty rash,

On cheap liquor his takings were spent.

A young couple quite clearly in love

Truly blessed loved the good lord above.

But he watched too much porn,

Now her anus is torn,

And looks awfully like a foxglove.

Master baker with quite tasty wares

Rather handsome the ladies would stare

As his buns were most round

And his baguette quite profound,

His iced finger was extraordinaire.

Kinky couple, seems they had forgotten

'Bout the vegies she'd placed in his bottom,

Quite uncomfy as hell

And my god what a smell,

Pretty nasty when they had turned rotten.

Once a couple in love but most chaste:

He to her: "love my seeds gone to waste

I wake up in the night

Sticky mess, pj's tight,

God won't mind if you have just a taste."

Bereaved shepherd who loved his wife dearly,

When she passed, took the loss quite severely.

As he tended his flock

They reacted with shock

He was lonely it seems, rather clearly.

Patient bloke, for 'the one' he was waiting,

Spent his nights quite alone masturbating.

Past his prime with regret,

He went onto the net,

Bought himself a girlfriend, self-inflating.

Wealthy woman whose husband had strayed,

He enjoyed coital bliss with their maid.

Now she irons cleans n mends,

"He's on business" pretends

As she smashed in their heads with a spade.

Angry butcher whose marriage had soured

Killed his wife and her liver devoured.

Made a pie with her thighs,

And kebabs with her eyes,

Fried her heart lightly spiced, dipped and floured.

Swedish vet took a couple of kittens

Turned them into a pair of warm mittens.

Sewed his dogs into hats,

Made a scarf with 12 rats,

Perfect wares for cold winter conditions.

There's this virgin who'd never been kissed

Felt aggrieved at the things he had missed,

So went out on the town

A few shots he drank down,

Humped a tramp n got aids, rather pissed.

Once a big strapping copper called Andy

Saw his wife's thong n thought "That looks dandy".

He perfected the look

With a shave and a tuck

Now on weekends prefers to be brandy.

Insatiable chubber from Niece

Had a craving for lard, fat and grease,

A desire for cake,

For fried foods he did ache,

Now his stomach hangs down to his knees.

Tasty sausage fan Frankie Maloney

Had a craving for fresh made boloney

From pigs' trotters and snout

Chicken's anus and trout

And some testicles, preferable pony.

Epileptic priest enjoys hot carnal feeling

And found celibacy quite unappealing.

Touched himself, had a seizure,

Like a Yellowstone geyser

Ejaculated and splattered the ceiling.

There's this butcher, finds piglets appealing

Turns him on, curly tails and hot squealing.

How it makes him flip out

When he touches their snout

Rubs their bellies, gets hot at the feeling.

This big drinker with legs crooked and bowed

Staggered drunk late one night down the road

When he started to vomit

Got flung over a bonnet

And a semi squished him like a toad.

Once a cock mad na-tu-rist called mike

Bought himself a quite fab dildo bike.

Grinning, rides through the grass

As it pummels his ass.

Likes it dry, but use lube if you like.

This big buggery fan from near Peking

One day woke found his sphincter was leaking.

Used a cork from some rum

Rammed it straight up his bum

Worked a treat, when it walked made a squeaking.

Once a grocer consumed with dark greed

Rubbed bananas when he had the need

Squeezed his nuts, groped his plums

Slid courgettes twixt his buns.

Watermelon? He swallows the seed.

A new love, mid act of sweet love making,

Said "Babe yeah so hot, god I'm shaking."

"Not a chance" she replied

"You don't touch either side

Now get off 'cos I'm done with my faking."

Keen geologist thrilled by erosion

Ox bow lakes, sedimentary corrosion

Quite turned on by ablation

Or a wet river basin

Limestone layers cause trouser explosion.

Lonely farmer, long nights, all alone

Watched hot animal vids on his phone

He succumbed to desire

As lambs set him afire

And the squealing pigs so made him moan.

This old seldom clothed grocer from Bude

Loved to dance outside schools in the nude.

Now he's locked up in jail

As he can't afford bail

And does jigs for smokes, phone cards and food.

An ex vegan, aroused by raw liver

And my word how fresh tripe made her shiver,

Sweet breads made her quite hot.

Offal? Creams on the spot!

A fresh snout made her moist and legs quiver.

Hope you feel better soon, hear you're hurting,

That your tummy's upset, shit's been squirting,

And the bed's rather soiled,

Sheets will need to be boiled,

Disinfect the walls, carpet and skirting.

Lonely bloke who lived south of the border

Placed a custom job, sex doll web order.

Tiny mouth, googly eyes,

Nipples large, like pork pies,

A big butt 'cos he like his girls broader.

A carnivorous chap from Tobruk

On the toilet he quivered and shook

For he would not eat greens

Fibre, roughage or beans,

And my god such a long time he took.

An adventurous husband each Friday

Would eat cock, 'twas his sexual bi-day,

Through the rest of the week

Mostly pussy he'd seek

Though each Wednesday was anus cream pie day.

Once a crossdressing builder from Dorset

Loved to squeeze himself into a corset.

He would tape up his bits

Wear a fake pair of tits

But still build you a wall, fix a faucet.

There's this hairy young lady called Betty

When aroused became musty and sweaty.

She'd be down on all fours

As it oozed from her pores

Wet and matted, hair hung like spaghetti.

About the Author

Malcolm C. Michaels can oft be found somewhere in Yorkshire at the edge of a rugby pitch fighting off the urge to be inappropriate. Poetically at least.

He was born in Hull, raised in South Africa and served time in a number of interesting places along the bank of the Humber before settling in Halifax via Sheffield.

Neither well educated nor particularly well read, his days are spent mostly in banking trying to remember just how he got there and realising it is probably far too late to do anything of note so why bother.

He has a fabulous family, a long-suffering wife and two wonderful boys, and there are a couple of cats who he swears only use him for body warmth, but that's okay.

oh, and he is not at all a fan of punctuation,

To find out more visit his website at http://afterwards.blog

Printed in Great Britain
by Amazon

59556374R00064